www.mascotbooks.com

For more information, please contact:
Mascot Books
P.O. Box 220157
Chantilly, VA 20153-0157
info@mascotbooks.com

CPSIA Code: PRT0811A
ISBN: 1-936319-71-3
ISBN-13: 978-1-936319-71-8

Printed in the United States

GROWING UP BUCKEYE

GRAYSON VISITS THE HORSESHOE

Brent Saneholtz

illustrated by
Cheri Nowack

"For Joy, Greyson, and Rowen."

~ Brent Saneholtz

On a bright and sunny Thursday afternoon, Grayson's Dad brought home three tickets to Saturday's Ohio State football game. Grayson was thrilled for his first trip to a Buckeye football game, but there was a lot of work that needed to be done before Grayson and his family could tailgate and have fun at the big game.

Friday morning, Grayson went to the grocery store with his Mom. As always, Grayson wanted to sit in the cart where all the food goes. His Mom bought a lot of tasty food for the tailgate, like chicken wings, hot dogs, bratwursts, chips, and other snack foods. There was barely enough room in the cart for Grayson to sit!

When Mom and Grayson came home, Grayson helped put all of the food away in its proper place. Mom started to make some of tomorrow's food while Grayson played with his favorite toys. One of Grayson's favorite snacks was a cheeseball, and Mom decorated one to look like a football!

Grayson's Dad needed to pack a cooler and a few games into the car for the tailgate, so he asked for Grayson's help. While Grayson packed bottles of water, juice boxes, and cans of soda into the cooler, Dad packed boards for corn-hole into the car. "Grayson, can you pack the corn-hole bags in the car when you're done with the cooler?," Dad asked. "Sure thing, Dad," answered Grayson. Grayson really liked helping Dad pack for the tailgate.

A little later, Mom called Grayson's Uncle Austin and Aunt Christy and invited them to the tailgate. Grayson also wanted his Dad to invite some of his friends. Grayson especially liked Dad's friends Goofy Greg, Fun Darin, and Clumsy Dan. Grayson always had fun with them.

After a long day of shopping, cooking, and packing for the tailgate, Mom, Dad, and Grayson were ready for bed. Grayson took a bath, brushed his teeth, and went potty before snuggling into bed. Grayson needed a good night's sleep to have enough energy to make it through the tailgate and football game.

The next morning, Grayson was so excited about his first tailgate and Ohio State football game that he woke up before his Mom and Dad. Grayson put on his favorite Buckeye football jersey, jeans, and socks and was ready to go!

After getting dressed and ready to go, Grayson sprinted into Mom and Dad's bedroom and yelled, "Wake up! Wake up! It's time to tailgate and watch the Buckeyes play football in the Horseshoe!"

In the kitchen, Mom cooked Grayson his favorite breakfast; cheesy eggs, bacon, toast with strawberry jam, and a tall glass of orange juice. Grayson knew he needed to eat a big breakfast to give him an energetic start to the day.

While Mom was getting ready for their big Buckeye adventure, Grayson and Dad packed the car with all of the delicious food, drinks, and fun games.

Just as Grayson, Mom and Dad arrived at the tailgate spot, Uncle Austin and Aunt Christy pulled up next to them. Uncle Austin, Dad, and Grayson set up the tables, chairs, and games while Mom and Aunt Christy put out the food.

Shortly after Mom finished putting out the food, Dad's friends Goofy Greg, Fun Darin, and Clumsy Dan stopped by. Clumsy Dan started to eat some buffalo wings, and it didn't take long until he spilled wing sauce all over his face and white Ohio State football jersey. Sometimes Grayson laughed when Clumsy Dan spilled something on himself.

After everyone had eaten enough food, Mom and Aunt Christy put the leftovers back in the car. Meanwhile, Grayson and Dad put some recyclables into a blue bag while Uncle Austin and Clumsy Dan were putting away the trash. While putting a plate into the trash bag, Clumsy Dan tripped on a water bottle and fell onto Uncle Austin. Clumsy Dan spilled ketchup all over Uncle Austin's jeans, and Uncle Austin was not happy!

With all of the leftover food, drinks, and games put away,
Mom, Dad, and Grayson said goodbye to Uncle Austin, Aunt
Christy, Goofy Greg, Fun Darin, and Clumsy Dan. Mom, Dad,
and Grayson walked briskly to St. John Arena to watch
The Ohio State University Marching Band practice
for their halftime performance. This practice
was called Skull Session, and Grayson liked
watching the sousaphone players.

Grayson really liked seeing the band play at Skull Session, but it was time to hurry over to Ohio Stadium so they could get to their seats in time to see the band enter Ohio Stadium.

Just after Mom, Dad, and Grayson arrived at their seats, the Drum Major led The Ohio State University Marching Band onto the field to perform "Script Ohio."

The crowd cheered loudly as the sousaphone player dotted the "I" and the band members completed "Script Ohio." Grayson clapped so loudly that his hands started to hurt!

Once the football game started, Grayson was really enjoying it. The Buckeyes scored touchdown after touchdown and the Buckeye defense dominated their rival team.

The Buckeyes won the football game in convincing fashion, outscoring the rival team 42 – 6. Some of the Ohio State players even poured a water-cooler on their coach!

After a long day of tailgating and watching the Buckeyes win the big game, Grayson was ready for bed. For Grayson, it was time to sleep and have sweet dreams about playing football for the Buckeyes someday.

The End.